E TRIPP

Tripp, Nathaniel

Snow comes to the farm

SNOW

comes to the farm

SNOW
comes to the farm

Nathaniel Tripp

illustrated by Kate Kiesler

CANDLEWICK PRESS
CAMBRIDGE, MASSACHUSETTS

To my mother, who continues to inspire me with her own
fascination with weather.

N. T.

For Tim and Becca and Linden Farm.

K. K.

Our farm is in a valley, all by itself.
It is like living on an island, surrounded by woods and sky.
In the autumn the wild geese fly overhead.
Their song is both happy and sad, and I begin to wish for snow.

There is one snow I'll always remember.

Winter had come.
     The bare trees and gray hills said so.
The frozen ground and ice on the pond said so.
     And the geese said so, as the cold weather chased them south.

Our cellar was filled with jars and baskets and bins of food.
     Our barn was filled with hay.
Frost feathers began to grow on my bedroom window overnight.
     In the mornings I looked out, hoping the snow had finally come.

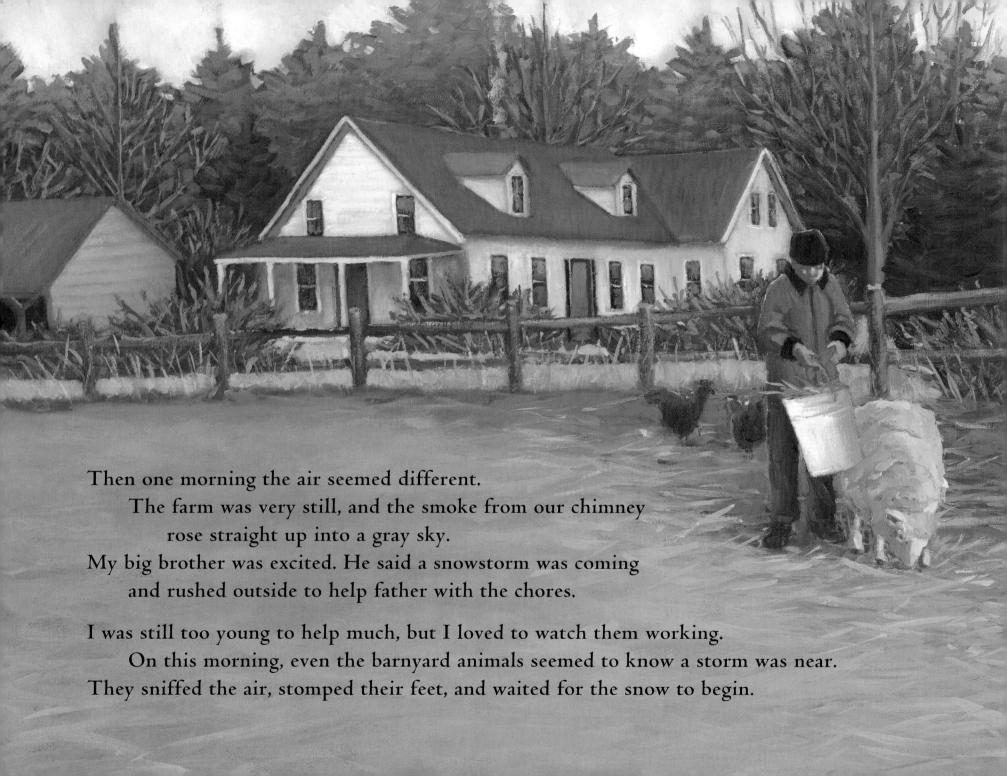

Then one morning the air seemed different.
  The farm was very still, and the smoke from our chimney
      rose straight up into a gray sky.
My big brother was excited. He said a snowstorm was coming
  and rushed outside to help father with the chores.

I was still too young to help much, but I loved to watch them working.
  On this morning, even the barnyard animals seemed to know a storm was near.
They sniffed the air, stomped their feet, and waited for the snow to begin.

Then, when the chores were done, my brother asked Father
    if he could take me up to the owl woods.
We could make a fire in the shelter of the tall pines.
    We'd watch the storm come, and maybe see the owl, too.
Father agreed, and Mother made us sandwiches
    while my little sister watched.
The sky grew darker, and finally it was time to go.

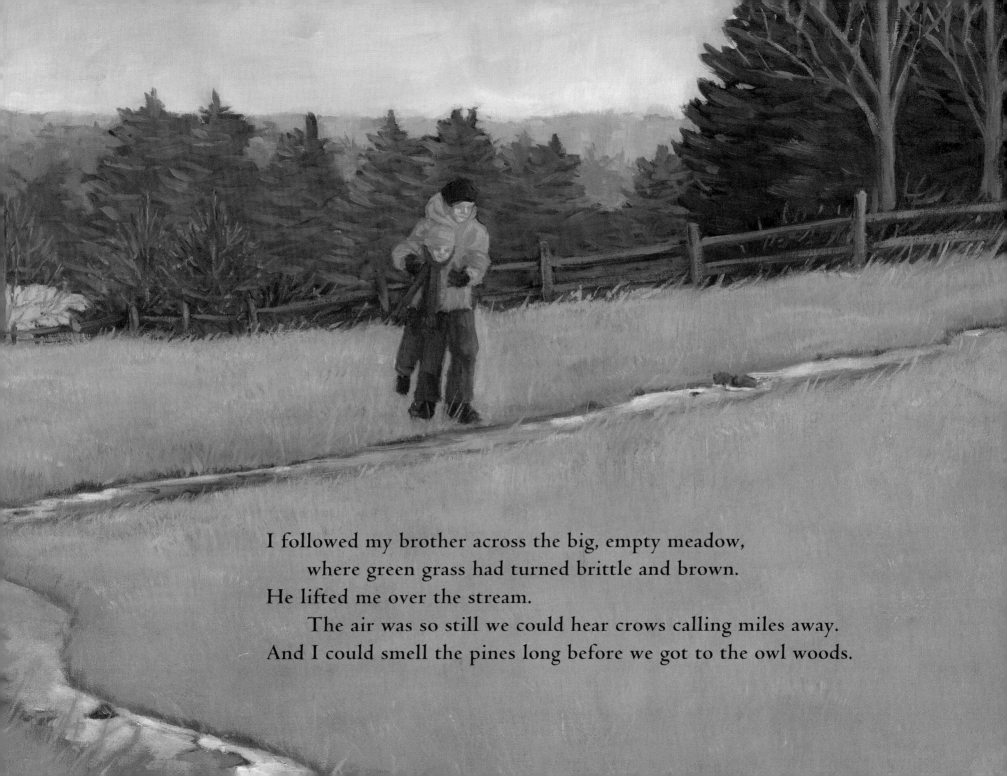

I followed my brother across the big, empty meadow,
   where green grass had turned brittle and brown.
He lifted me over the stream.
      The air was so still we could hear crows calling miles away.
And I could smell the pines long before we got to the owl woods.

My brother carefully cleared a safe place for a fire.
    We gathered pine needles and dry twigs.
Soon, smoke rose through the branches above us.
    We waited, warmed our hands, and ate the sandwiches.
Where was the snow?

Then at last we saw the first snowflakes.
 Just a little glitter, floating in the air.

I was disappointed.
 But my brother told me to keep waiting. . . .
The biggest storms begin with the smallest flakes.

I waited, smelled pines, listened to the crows.
 Then the crows became silent.

The flakes were falling faster.
They were bigger now, too.
We could hear them whisper as they brushed
against the branches, and see their shapes
like little stars on our sleeves.

We got down on our hands and knees to watch them land.
One by one, the flakes filled the cups of fallen leaves.
Then they spilled over and covered everything.
The ground turned white. The hills faded away.

All through the woods, mice and squirrels bustled about,
    leaving snowy footprints as they gathered food for the storm.
We knew that the owl was sleeping somewhere above us.
    And later, after dark, after we went home, the deer would come.

Then waves of snow poured through the woods, more and more and more.
    Every twig wore a coat of white, and the trees looked like frost feathers.

We saw the owl!
    Silent as the smoke from our fire,
        he glided through the trees and away into the storm.

I felt the wind, like the storm's heavy breathing.
   Tree branches sagged lower, heavy with snow.
The flakes hissed and stung our cheeks.

Even the fire couldn't keep us warm anymore.
   Darkness was coming.
My brother put the fire out.
   Darkness surrounded us.

My brother took my hand in his and began to lead us back.
Snow swirled across the path and quickly covered our tracks.
Piles of snow slid down on us from the trees.
But my brother's hand was warm and strong, and
I could see the orange lights of our farmhouse.

The storm blew harder as we crossed the meadow.
   The wind piled drifts behind fences, tugged our clothes, and moaned.
Through the kitchen window, I saw my father, and mother, and sister by the stove.

We were the last ones home,
   long after evening chores were done.
We sipped hot cocoa and told everyone what we had seen,
   while our mittens dried by the cook stove
      and the snow brushed against the windowpanes.

The storm would huff and blow all night,
   but it began to whisper sleep to us.
So we went upstairs and pulled the blankets over us.
   I promised my sister she could come with us next time.

Outside the snow kept falling like owl down.

Text copyright © 2001 by Nathaniel Tripp
Illustrations copyright © 2001 by Kate Kiesler

First edition 2001

Library of Congress Cataloging-in-Publication Data

Tripp, Nathaniel.
Snow comes to the farm / Nathaniel Tripp ;
illustrated by Kate Kiesler. — 1st ed.

p.   cm.

Summary: During a snowstorm, a farm child goes to the woods
to watch the ground turn white, observe animal tracks,
and spot an owl gliding through the trees.

ISBN 1-56402-426-1

[1. Snow—Fiction. 2. Storms—Fiction. 3. Nature—Fiction.
4. Farm life—Fiction.] I. Kiesler, Kate, ill. II. Title.

PZ7.T73574 Sn 2001
[E]—dc21 99-057128

2 4 6 8 10 9 7 5 3 1

Printed in Italy

This book was typeset in Centaur.
The illustrations were done in oils.

Candlewick Press
2067 Massachusetts Avenue
Cambridge, Massachusetts 02140

visit us at www.candlewick.com